My grateful thanks to all the peaceful people I know, but especially to
Katharina Gasterstadt, Gianluca Manna, Iolanda Bellone
at B-side studio in Rome.

Atheneum Books for Young Readers · An imprint of Simon & Schuster Children's Publishing Division
1230 Avenue of the Americas · New York, New York 10020
Copyright © 2002 by Vladimir Radunsky
Book design by Vladimir Radunsky. Prepress and coccole by B-Side Studio Grafico, Roma.
All text is set in BauerBodoni. The illustrations are rendered in prezzemolo on paper. First Edition. Printed in Hong Kong
1 2 3 4 5 6 7 8 9 10 Library of Congress Control Number: 2001094692
ISBN 0-689-83193-5

MANNEKEN Pis

A simple story of a boy
who peed on a war.

As told by Vladimir Radunsky

An Anne Schwartz Book
Atheneum Books for Young Readers

New York   London   Toronto   Sydney   Singapore

A long, long time ago, there behind a tall stone wall. It

was a small, beautiful town

looked like this.

In this town lived a little boy
with his mother and father.

His parents loved him madly.

Mother kissed him
all the time,

and Father
played with him
all day long.

Every morning the little boy
went with his Father and Mother
to the flower market.
Oh, what beautiful flowers.

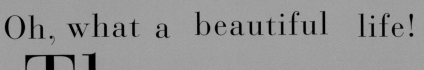

Oh, what a beautiful life!
They were so happy.

But then   something   happened.

The War.

Enemies   came to destroy the beautiful town.

Maybe they were jealous
that the town was so beautiful.

Oh, what a terrible, terrible war.

And the big fight began.
They fought
and fought.

Day and night, day and night.

What a small, sad town.

No more playing in the streets.
No more flowers in the market.

No more laughing anywhere.

The little boy grew sad.

There was no father to play with him,
no mother to kiss him.

Where did they go?

He called and called, but nobody came.

The boy looked and looked.
But all he saw was fighting
everywhere, even right on the town wall.

All he heard was
Bang-Bang,
Boom-Boom,

Cling-Clang.
Poor little boy, he was scared.
He needed his mother and father.

But more than that he needed . . .

. . . to pee. He could not wait any more and . . .

he peed right there.

Down onto the Booms and Bangs and Cling-Clangs he peed.

He peed to the left, then to the right.

Please forgive him. He was just a little boy.

Suddenly everything

was still.

Then somebody laughed,
ha- ha- ha-ha-ha
Then,
ho-ho-ho-ho-ho-ho-ho.

Then,

he- he- he.
he- he-

And before long, all around the tall town wall
was laughing, laughing, laughing.

On and on it went, until the sun had set
and the first star came out, and the people
had grown so tired laughing that they
dropped their arms and went to sleep.

When they woke up the next morning,
there was no more war. Why?
Because of that wonderful, wonderful little boy.

Hurra-a

-a-ah!!!!

EpiLogue

And of course the little boy found his Mother and Father.
   Oh, it was heaven on earth!

They were so happy again.

All the people in the town loved the little boy.
And they decided to make a bronze statue of him
so that their children and even their grandchildren would
remember him forever. The little boy who peed on a war.

And they named the statue

Manneken Pis,

which means "peeing boy."

This all happened a long time ago in the town named

Brussels,

in the country named

Belgium.

I hope one day you go there and see this statue
with your own eyes.
And now you know the whole story
and can tell it to your children, and they will tell it
to their children, and their children will tell it to their
children, and so on, and so on.

The End